DON'T TELL ME NO

HONEY CHANEL

Copyright © 2021 by Honey Chanel

Cover Design by Honey Chanel

Edited by Dana Hook with Rebel Edit & Design.

All rights reserved.

This is a work of fiction. Names, characters, organizations, businesses, events, and incidents are a figment of the author's imagination and are used fictitiously. Any similarities to real people, businesses, locations, history, and events are a coincidence.

All rights reserved.

No part of this publication may be reproduced, distributed, or transmitted in any form or by any means, including photocopying, recording, or other electronic or mechanical methods, without the prior written permission of the publisher.

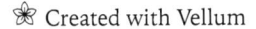

✤ Created with Vellum

Don't Tell Me No was previously featured in the Girls Night anthology.

BLURB

All debts must be paid. No matter the cost...

Raya White was payment for her husband's crimes. The thief had pawned her off to his billionaire boss to pay back the money he had embezzled. Unknowingly, she was an accomplice, living off the false wealth she'd thought he'd earned.

Backed into a corner, she has no choice but to submit to pay the debt.

The word 'no' was no longer able to be in her vocabulary.

What started out as a sentence, turned into so much more.

She fell for the woman.

Craved her.

Now she doesn't want to leave.

WARNING

This book is pure lesbian erotica. Hot, steamy sex will fill the following pages. If you are looking for characters with much depth and a full length novel—this isn't the book for you.

Looking for a hot reads of a husband using his wife as payment, then this is the book for you! Enjoy it and make sure you leave a review after reading!

Honey Chanel

CHAPTER 1

Holding the suitcase that held her belongings, her hand trembled. "Are you sure there's no other way?" Raya asked her husband of five years, Brandon, who was standing in the doorway. Her husband worked as an Executive Financial Officer—well, used to work—for Hamilton Technologies, until he was caught embezzling a couple million dollars from the company.

And she was deemed an accomplice.

Apparently, she knew what her thief of a husband had been doing. It was guilty by association.

She'd met him when she was nineteen years old, and his smooth-talking, frat boy persona had captivated her. They'd dated all through college and got married once they had graduated.

It could have been called a fairy tale courting.

Raya came from an average blue-collared family. Her parents, Nick and Lorna Martinez, had worked hard to put her through college. Brandon, on the other hand, came from a well-off family, and got into college on a lacrosse scholarship.

It was almost like fate had played a part in their meeting. They didn't run in the same crowds. She wasn't into sports much. She was an English major, while he was in finance.

She'd only attended the party at his fraternity house because her roommate had been dating a member.

She remembered the night they'd met. He had been dressed in jeans and a blue cotton T-shirt that highlighted his muscular physique, while also enhancing his eyes. He'd offered to get her a drink, and she had been tongue-tied from the moment he'd set his sights on her.

A jock and frat boy were interested in her, a mousy girl with big brown eyes and dark hair.

She wasn't some girl who chased after the jocks.

She was known to hang out in the library, writing, or with her nose deep in a book.

One drink that night had cascaded into a full-on romance.

They had been inseparable after that.

So, to hear that her husband had stolen millions of dollars from his employer was quite baffling.

Raya thought she knew him.

This was quite out of character for him.

He sighed. "If there was, don't you think I would have done it by now?"

"How about you shouldn't have taken money that wasn't yours to begin with!" she cried out, running a hand through her dark hair as she walked over to the window of their bedroom.

The beautifully landscaped yard was a prized possession of hers. She had taken great care in ensuring their yard was attractive and welcoming.

Now, staring out at the property, a sour taste appeared in her mouth.

It was created from stolen money.

While her husband was climbing the

ranks at Hamilton Technologies, she had had a blossoming writing career.

She was a best-selling writer who wrote mystery and suspense novels, with a very strong following. Alone, she could easily support the two of them comfortably, but Brandon had wanted to be the breadwinner.

They had no children. They had wanted to wait until around thirty to do so, with the thought of enjoying each other and becoming well-established before expanding their family.

"Look, I'm sorry. This is the only way she wouldn't press charges and have me arrested. We'd lose everything we have." He came to stand behind her, and she stiffened at the sensation of his hands resting on her shoulders.

Her vision blurred with unshed tears. Raya had never been so pissed in her life.

"So, you get to avoid jail while I have to live as a woman's sex slave?" She spun around and glared up at him, wiping the tears from her cheeks.

A pain-filled expression fluttered across his face.

"You don't know that that's what she

wants from you." He scrubbed his hands over his haggard looking face, and was still wearing the clothes he'd slept in the night before. "Maybe she wants to use your writing skills to write a book for her or something. Why would you automatically jump to sex slave?"

There were some things Raya had chosen not to tell Brandon over the years.

She'd been around his ex-boss before at company functions.

Hadley Hamilton was a powerful woman who never hid her feelings, nor did she bite her tongue. There were plenty of occasions when she told Raya that she was beautiful, or liked the way something looked on Raya. The woman always commented on her curvy frame.

The woman's eyes said it all.

She lusted after Raya.

Flirted with her every chance she got.

Raya never mentioned any of this to Brandon because she didn't want to make him feel uncomfortable since he worked for her.

How would she have said it anyway?

Your boss, who is a very wealthy and powerful woman, keeps coming on to me?

Instead, Raya had chosen to remain silent.

"So while I'm off being used only God knows how, what will you be doing?" Folding her arms across her chest, she leaned back against the windowsill.

"I'll be looking for new employment. I'm going to fix this. I'll get a job where we'll be able to maintain our lifestyle, and we won't have to use your savings."

Raya closed her eyes. She couldn't believe she was doing this.

But what other choice did she have?

If Hadley reported this to the police, they could both be facing serious jail time.

"What time do we have to be there?" she whispered.

"We're to meet with her in her office at six."

Raya glanced at the clock on the nightstand. Less than an hour.

"Then I guess I better finish getting ready."

Raya sat silently in the passenger seat of her husband's luxury vehicle while he drove them to his old office building downtown. Her stomach was tied up in knots. She felt as if she were reporting to prison.

Brandon may not be going to jail, but she was.

She was to pay for his crimes.

A debt must be paid, and the payment was Raya.

The agreement between Hadley and Brandon was that he would resign from his position. Though a few of his colleagues knew about his thievery, she would sweep it under the rug if he gave Raya to her.

That part of the deal, no one else knew about.

"It's going to be okay." Brandon reached out and took her hand in his. "Time will fly by, and before you know it, you will be home with me." He kissed the back of her hand.

She tried to offer him a small smile, because deep down, she knew he felt helpless. He hadn't slept in days, trying to find ways to liquidate some of their assets to pay the company back, but Hadley hadn't wanted money.

She wanted Raya.

"Will I be able to speak with you?" she asked.

"I don't know, baby, but we'll ask her." He pressed another kiss to her hand. "I love you. You know that, right?"

He turned a hopeful gaze in her direction before focusing back on the road.

"Yeah. I love you too," Raya murmured, tightening her grip on his hand as she watched the scenery fly by. Though she could barely concentrate on it, for she didn't know what exactly she was walking into.

Soon, they arrived at the downtown skyscraper.

There was some traffic on the streets, but most people must have left work early to begin their weekend, being that it was Friday.

Brandon guided the car into the underground garage for executives and parked before turning to her.

"Come here." He gathered her to him in a tight hug. Raya closed her eyes and held on to him.

I will not cry, she chanted in her head.

"I don't want to go." Her voice was muffled as she breathed in his familiar scent. It was the cologne she'd purchased for him a few Christmases ago, and it always comforted her when she was sad about something.

"I know, baby, I fucked up. But I promise I'll make this up to you." He pulled back and cupped her cheeks in his hand. Leaning forward, he pressed a gentle kiss to her lips. "Let's go. We can't keep her waiting."

Sniffing, Raya nodded.

Exiting the car, Brandon came around to her side and assisted her out before going to the trunk. Raya hefted the strap of her purse up on her shoulder and strolled to the back of the car.

One suitcase.

That's what she would be living out of until she returned home.

Brandon took her hand and entwined their fingers, guiding her through the entrance while dragging her wheeled suitcase and carrying her computer bag. She held onto him as if her life depended on it.

With it being after hours, the building was like walking through a ghost town.

Her heels echoed across the marble floor as they arrived at the elevator. The doors opened immediately, and Brandon ushered her inside, hitting the top floor button as the doors closed.

Classical music filled the car.

It did nothing to settle her nerves.

The two of them remained quiet.

Raya was trying to not panic.

She would be strong for them both.

Once they arrived at the top floor, Brandon guided her through the office layout, where they came to a private sector in the back. The desk where Raya assumed a secretary sat was empty. Behind the desk were the words *Hamilton Technologies* in bold, steel letters bolted to the wall.

The area was elegant, and screamed money. This was where the president and CEO of the company worked.

"No one is here," Raya breathed.

Brandon shook his head. "She's here."

He walked over to a set of sturdy, ostentatious wooden doors, and Raya followed behind him slowly while her heart raced.

Doubt clouded her mind. She didn't know if she could go through with this.

Brandon turned and took hold of her hand.

"Six months will go by fast. Then you'll come home, and we'll move on with our lives," he told her.

She didn't say a word.

Pressing a kiss to her forehead, he rapped his knuckles against the door.

"Come in." The voice was muffled, but Raya heard it clear as day.

Brandon turned the knob and opened the door.

CHAPTER 2

Hadley Hamilton sat regally in her oversized leather chair, a wall of windows stretched out behind her. Her blonde hair flowed down around her shoulders, her blue eyes icy as she watched Brandon and Raya enter her office.

Raya's heart slammed against her chest.

This was it.

She was actually going to go through with this.

She was turning herself over to this woman.

Raya swallowed hard, following her husband across the vast, tastefully decorated office. One wall displayed leather-bound books and plaques along numerous shelves, while the other was decorated with expensive artwork. The office had a seating area off to the side with two couches, and a television mounted on the wall over a large fireplace.

Hadley pushed back from the desk and stood.

"Greetings." Her voice was husky, almost seductive. Raya remembered joking once about Brandon's employer's voice, asking if she was a smoker. Surprisingly, Brandon said the woman had never picked up a cigarette. "Brandon. Raya, how are you?"

Hadley walked around the desk and met them. Her gaze landed on Brandon, her look cold and calculated.

"We're doing as well as can be," Brandon replied, then cleared his throat as he glanced nervously at Raya. He had finally taken a shower before they left. He was dressed business casual, consisting of slacks and a button-down shirt.

Hadley's attention turned to Raya, and she tightened her grip on Brandon's hand, where Hadley's gaze dropped down to.

"Hmm…" Hadley turned back to her desk and shuffled through some papers. "Raya will need to sign a contract."

"Wait. What contract?" Raya asked, finally

finding her voice. She was confused. Why would she need to sign a contract?

"That's how all business ventures should be handled." Hadley turned back around with the paperwork in her hand.

"Sounds fair. I'm sure it will be all right," Brandon murmured in Raya's ear. "She never backs down from a contract or promise."

He pulled back and turned to Hadley, who handed the contract to Raya. "I'm sure you'll find that it's fair and covers all parties." Taking it, she gripped it in her hand and blew out a deep breath, her eyes skimming the few pages.

Short and to the point.

It was a contract covering travel, sleeping arrangements, and sex.

She swallowed hard at the section that spoke of sexual activities.

She continued on until she was finished. It put Raya in a position to be at Hadley's beck and call in order to pay off the debt owed to the company. If she completed the six months, then no charges would be filed.

If she didn't, the police would be notified, and they would be prosecuted to the full extent of the law.

Raya's eyes narrowed in on one clause.

She would need to remove the word *no* from her vocabulary.

"I'm sorry, but I need clarification on this. What does section four, article two mean?" As she looked up from the papers, Brandon took them from her and cursed as he read through it.

"As it states, *no* is not a word that will be used between you and I," Hadley calmly explained. "I promise, no harm will come to you while you are in my care." Her lips turned up slightly. "But I do plan for you to enjoy yourself while you're with me."

Brandon handed Raya the papers back, taking a few steps away from her, running his hands through his hair. Raya was concerned that soon, he'd go bald from the habit.

"So I'm never allowed to use the word?" Raya scanned down farther on the page and caught sight of a line where she could choose a safe word.

"If you look, you'll see where you can choose to use a safe word if you're uncomfortable with anything." Hadley stood there in her tailored business suit, and it was at that moment Raya recognized the shrewd businesswoman she was.

"There has to be another way," Brandon muttered.

Hadley narrowed her gaze on him. "There is. I call the police, you get arrested, and then I press charges. I have very deep pockets, Brandon, way beyond the two million dollars you stole from me."

"I'll sign it," Raya chirped, not wanting the woman to change her mind. It was six months of her life that she was signing over to her. The only thing comforting her at the moment was the ability to use a safe word to stop anything.

Brandon turned to her, anger filling his eyes.

"I'll sign it," she repeated, softer.

Hadley held out a silver fountain pen.

Brushing past Brandon, Raya took the pen from the billionaire. Setting her purse on the desk, she placed the papers beside it and stared at the documents.

"I assure you, Brandon, no harm will come to your wife. Two million dollars is a lot of money to repay. This is an easy out for the both of you," Hadley stated.

"Raya didn't have anything to do—"

"You expect me to believe that? Husbands and wives talk all the time. She lived in your fancy house, drove your expensive cars," Hadley snapped.

Raya scribbled her name on the line at the bottom, signing her life away.

Six months of her life was worth two million dollars.

But anger simmered inside of her. Due to her husband's greed, her life now had a monetary value to it.

Her gaze darted again to the safe word. She thought for a moment, chewing on her bottom lip. One of her favorite animals came to mind.

Elephant.

She wrote the word out and stepped back.

"It's done." Raya glanced at Brandon, then ran a hand along his face.

"Good." Hadley stepped over, picked up the pen, and signed her name below Raya's. "I will have my secretary issue you a copy of the contract for you to maintain for your records."

"Will I be able to speak to my husband?" Raya asked.

Pausing, she met Raya's gaze before jerking her head. "Once a week. Sundays at noon for no more than thirty minutes."

Raya blew out a deep breath.

It was something.

"Thank you," Raya murmured. She didn't know if she should be depressed or angry.

Her tone sharp, Hadley ordered, "Brandon, I'll need your badge."

Raya expected nothing less, seeing as he'd stolen millions from her company.

When he looked over at her and swallowed hard, reality hit. She had just signed her life over to this woman because of him. Could she forgive him? If she did, it would take some time. This wasn't something she could ignore by morning like any other arguments they'd had.

This was more than discovering he'd eaten the rest of her Oreos.

Heavy footsteps thudded across the floor, away from her. She stiffened until she heard the door open and shut.

He was gone.

Slumping her shoulders, she released the breath she hadn't realized she was holding.

"Well, now, it's time for us to go." Suddenly, Hadley was standing before her, and gently tilted Raya's head back. The woman was significantly taller than her, especially in heels, where she topped at least six feet tall. Her blue eyes seemed to bore into hers. "It won't be so bad. You'll see. Come."

Hadley walked away and grabbed her belongings while Raya snagged her purse from the desk, grabbed her suitcase, and followed Hadley out through a secret door that led to an elevator.

This was it.

At twenty-eight years old, she officially belonged to the billionaire businesswoman.

What had she done?

A PRIVATE CAR WAS WAITING FOR them when they exited the building. Raya was nervous about being near Hadley; they had never been alone together before. She settled back against the plush leather seats and stared out the window, the quiet ride somewhat uncomfortable. She recognized the area they were driving through. It was a gated community in a pricey neighborhood.

The driver guided the vehicle to a fantastic mansion that overlooked a cliff showcasing the Pacific Ocean. The grounds were meticulously decorated and beautiful.

"Welcome to my home," Hadley purred.

Raya cleared her throat. "It's beautiful."

Bringing the car to a halt, the driver stepped out and opened Haley's door. Once she exited, he shut it, allowing Raya a moment to take a deep breath. She gripped the handle of her purse tight to keep from trembling.

Then her door opened. She looked over to see the driver holding his hand out for her.

"Thank you." She took it and stepped out.

"Follow me. I'll give you the tour," Hadley offered.

Raya followed behind her as they walked up to the front door, where they were greeted by a butler who tipped his head.

"Good evening, Ms. Hamilton."

"Ian, this is Raya White. She'll be my guest for the next few months."

"Mrs. White, nice to meet you." The older man held out his hand, and Raya took it in a firm shake.

"Likewise," Raya murmured.

"Shall you be dining tonight?" He asked after he shut the door.

"I'm sure Raya will be tired and wanting to get settled in. We can take our supper in our rooms."

Raya relaxed at the notion of having her own room.

"Of course, ma'am." Tipping his head once again, he moved down the grand hallway.

"I promised you a tour. Don't worry about your things, they'll be placed in your bedroom." They fell into step together. "You may have full access of the house and the yard. I'm sure you will love the gardens and the pool. There is much to do on this property. Outside of the telephone call to your husband on Sundays, there will be no outside contact with anyone."

"Okay." She had to think of something regarding her parents. They lived on the East Coast, so she didn't get to travel to see them as much as she wanted, but she and her mother spoke at least once a week. Raya didn't want to push Hadley by requesting something else, though, and decided to wait until later to bring it up.

"Anything you find you need, you can provide a list to my assistant. She will ensure you have everything you need here. I'm sure you read the contract. You will travel with me, and be at my beck and call. Again, you know which word you are never to utter to me."

She turned her attention to Raya.

"The word *no*."

"Let that be the last time you use it around me. Is that understood?"

The intensity of her stare sent a shiver down Raya's spine.

Reaching up, Raya tucked a wayward strand of hair behind her ear as she met the woman's steady gaze.

"Completely," she replied.

"Good." Hadley continued down the hall. "If there is ever something not pleasing to you, or hurts you in any way, then that is when your safe word is to come into play." She led Raya up to the second floor and down the hallway. Pausing outside of a room, she opened the door to reveal a large room with plenty of natural light coming in from the windows.

Raya walked inside and strolled around what was to be her private quarters for the next six months, which had all the necessities of home. A king-sized bed that looked extremely comfortable with plenty of pillows. Her suitcase and computer bag sat next to it.

An area with a desk where she could work was next to a set of sliding glass doors that led out to a veranda. The gardens were below her suite, and she already knew she would spend plenty of mornings outside smelling the fresh air, the ocean, and the flowers.

A gorgeous private en suite with a jacuzzi tub and separate shower completed the space.

"Here's your closet." Hadley opened the set of French doors and disappeared into the room. Raya followed her inside and paused. There were plenty of clothes, but it was the rows of lingerie that caught her attention. Her breath caught in her throat at all the fancy, lacy undergarments that were right up her alley. She loved sexy wear, and had plenty of her own at home, but she didn't have it in her to bring her own. All of what she collected was for Brandon's eyes only.

It looked like she wouldn't need it anyway.

"Wow," she whispered, turning around in a circle. It was a lot to take in. She'd owned a ton of clothes, but nothing to the level of what Hadley was providing her. The closet was the size of her old apartment in college. There were rows and rows of clothes, shoes, and accessories. "All of this is for me?"

Smirking, Hadley sauntered over to Raya and stopped in front of her, her gaze traveling the length of Raya's body. Raya had to fight not to squirm under the woman's heated stare.

"The lingerie will be your uniform when I call for you. That is what you are to wear in this house. Outside, or when we are out in public, you may wear clothing."

Raya nodded, her gaze landing on a door Hadley hadn't opened yet.

"Where does that lead?" she asked, pointing to it.

"My bedroom." Hadley smiled and closed the space between them. Reaching up, she trailed a finger along Raya's cheek. "We'll have fun together, my dear. I've thought of your body many, many times. You are such a beautiful woman. I shall take great pleasure in exploring you." Her finger arrived at Raya's lips.

Raya couldn't believe how her body trembled. It was as if she were under a spell.

Hadley's spell.

Her core clenched as Hadley slid her finger along Raya's bottom lip.

They parted ever so slightly.

"But not tonight." Dropping her hand to her side, Hadley stepped back, her infamous smirk back. The woman knew how she affected Raya, and from the glint in her eyes, she planned to have fun with it. "Unpack and settle in. We have plenty of time to get acquainted."

CHAPTER 3

Raya turned over in her plush bed, a deep breath escaping her as she stretched her legs and arms.

She'd slept surprisingly well.

At the delicious aroma of coffee teasing her nose, she opened her eyes to find a white porcelain mug sitting on the nightstand, the steam drifting into the air. She sat up, but didn't see anyone in the room.

Leaning back against her pillow, she brushed her long tresses away from her face and looked back to the nightstand, seeing a letter lying just next to the mug.

Nervous, she stared at it.

What would it say?

Raya grabbed the envelope and held it in her hand, the soft paper thick and expensive, smelling of lilac. On the front was her name, scrawled in bold lettering.

Opening it, she pulled the note out.

My Dearest Raya,

I've been called away for an important meeting. Enjoy the house, explore, and you'll have a treat for breakfast. Remember your uniform, and I'll see you at dinner.

Yours,

Hadley

She didn't know what to think of the letter. *My dearest Raya? Yours, Hadley?* What the hell did that mean?

She breathed in the scent of the perfume, finding it pleasing. Yawning, Raya stood from the bed and snagged the coffee, taking a small sip. It had been made just to her liking.

Whoever brought it was apparently psychic.

Coffee in hand, she walked over to the double doors that led out to the veranda and stepped out and onto the cold concrete porch. The sky was beautiful, bright, and free of clouds.

Raya leaned against the railing, looking out over the immaculate grounds and beyond to the cliff that led to the ocean.

The beautiful backdrop was inspiring. The writer in her was thinking of tales she could weave about a murder committed in a mansion. The cliff, the ocean, and the remote area would be the perfect setting for a new novel.

With a sigh, Raya tipped back her cup and finished off her coffee. It was good, but her stomach was now demanding nourishment.

"Time to find food," she muttered. As much as she wanted to stay and enjoy the morning out on the veranda, she would have to face reality and wander around the home.

Taking one more longing look at the ocean, she went back inside the house. A few minutes later, she had found a matching robe and slippers to put on and left her quarters in search of the kitchen.

On the first floor, she looked around, trying to remember landmarks from the previous night.

Finally, the smell of something sweet floated through the air, leading her in the right direction.

Raya hesitated in the doorway, taking in the kitchen of a cook's dreams. Large and spacious, with plenty of counter space and cabinets. All the appliances were top of the line.

The sunlight streamed in through the large windows, making it appear even brighter.

A short, stocky woman dressed in a chef's jacket and dark pants was fiddling around at the countertop. Her blonde hair was pulled up into a bun with a few strands escaping. Opening the large oven, she pulled out a tray of something that smelled delicious.

Raya's stomach rumbled.

"Good morning," Raya called out.

"Oh." The woman spun around with a tray in her hand. Upon seeing Raya, a smile spread across her lips. "Mrs. White. Good morning."

Raya wasn't sure if the house staff knew about her, but she shouldn't have been surprised the woman knew who she was.

"I hope I'm not bothering you. I'm in search of food." Raya laughed as the woman waved her into the kitchen.

"Well, you came to the right place. I'm Sue, the executive chef here."

Executive chef?

Fancy.

She walked over to the island and took a seat on one of the thickly padded stools, offering Sue a smile.

"Anything particular you would like? I can

whip you up some pancakes."

Raya's stomach chose that moment to growl. She covered her face, while Sue chuckled at her embarrassment.

"Whatever you've already made is fine." Raya's nose picked up the scent of cinnamon, and her mouth watered, wondering what deliciousness came out of the oven.

"Cinnamon rolls it is." Laughing, Sue pulled a plate out of the cabinet. "Fresh from the oven. You're just in time."

Her eyes landing on the coffee pot, she slid off her seat and padded over to it.

"Is that coffee fresh?"

"It is. Cups are right above in the cabinet. I can pour it if you'd like."

"Pfft. I can pour my own cup of coffee."

Sue chuckled. "You've got spunk."

Pouring a fresh cup, Raya settled back into her seat and found the biggest cinnamon roll she had ever seen sitting on a plate.

"Oh, my. I'm going to need to work out after eating this," Raya chuckled. Grabbing her fork, she dug in.

"There's a gym here in the house."

She took a bite of the sweet deliciousness in front of her.

"So, how long have you worked here?" Raya inquired.

"Oh, about ten years," Sue responded over her shoulder.

Raya grew curious. If the cook had been employed by Hadley that long, then she had to really know the billionaire. Taking the last bite, she set her fork down and sipped on her coffee.

"She doesn't usually bring people here," Sue informed her.

"She doesn't?"

Sue offered her a small smile. "Nope. You must be special."

"Not really." Raya lowered her head, not wanting to explain her reason for being there. "Well, whatever the reason, she must like you." Backing away, Sue walked over to the fridge and began making notes.

Raya continued to sip her coffee while Sue's words echoed in her head.

She doesn't usually bring people here.

What was so special about her, then?

"Breakfast was wonderful," Raya murmured as she rose from her seat and grabbed her plate.

"You can leave that there, honey. I'll get it."

"Are you sure?"

"Of course," Sue snorted. "Ms. Hadley will have my ass if she finds out you've lifted a finger." With a wide grin, she mentioned, "You're a writer, I hear."

"I am."

She had a word count she needed to hit today. With a new story brewing in her head, she had put herself on a self-imposed deadline.

Topping off her coffee, she waved as she headed out of the kitchen.

Raya stared at the black lace negligee that hugged her feminine curves in the mirror, paper-thin and delicate. Her areolas were completely visible, as the pretty dress didn't hide a thing.

She absolutely loved it.

Wrapping a dark silk gown around herself, she secured the ties. Dinner was at six. She had soaked in the oversized tub and scrubbed herself clean. She wasn't sure why her heart was racing, but she chalked it up to nerves and the unknown.

She left her thick, dark hair down, letting it flow past her shoulders, brushing it until it was silky smooth. Light make-up and lip gloss completed her look.

"It's just dinner," she muttered to herself.

Walking over to the closet, she took out a pair of dark Christian Louboutin shoes, the five-inch heel raising her to a good height.

If she wasn't too careful, she might start liking it here. She had a decent size closet at home, but it was nothing compared to the elegance and designer style of this.

Brandon always splurged, buying expensive name brands, while she was still getting used to them having money.

But here, she had no worries. Hadley was loaded, and if she wanted to blow money on her, who was she to say no?

Oops. Not supposed to use that word.

Jogging back to the mirror, she modeled the shoes with her sexy outfit. She barely recognized herself.

She glanced over at the clock on her nightstand and saw it was time for dinner.

"Let's get this over with."

Walking to the door, she couldn't help but note the extra sway in her hips. Raya didn't know if it was the heels doing it, or if she was actually looking forward to the dinner.

A knock sounded at the door. Turning the knob slowly, she opened it cautiously.

"Raya." Hadley stood in the hallway, looking radiant in a black cashmere crewneck dress. It complimented her bronze skin and blonde hair that hung around her shoulders. Her sharp blue eyes traveled down her body, leaving Raya feeling breathless.

"Hadley, how are you?" Raya asked, suddenly feeling shy. She swallowed hard, seeing that her added height was no competition for the five-inch heeled boots Hadley wore, topping her at over six feet.

Hadley took her hand and tugged her out into the hallway. "Much better now that I'm in your presence."

Raya closed the door behind her, mesmerized by Hadley's gaze. Her cheeks warmed at the intense attention of the billionaire.

Hadley brought Raya's hand up to her lips and pressed a kiss to her wrist.

"Beautiful."

"Thank you." Raya swallowed hard, her core clenching with need.

All from a single kiss to her skin.

She almost wanted to pull Hadley to her and demand a kiss.

"Come. I hear Sue really went above and beyond for dinner tonight." Entwining their fingers, she guided her toward the stairs.

Raya giggled. "Well, if it's as good as those rolls, then I can't wait."

"I told you that you were in for a treat. Sue is the best chef around. I have to keep her happy so she won't leave me for another rich employer," Hadley joked. Her laugh was deep, husky, and sent a tremor down her spine.

Raya paused at the top of the stairs and stared at Hadley.

"What's wrong, my love?" Reaching up, she brushed aside Raya's dark tresses from her face.

"I just realized that was the first time I've heard you laugh," Raya murmured. Out of all the years she'd known Hadley, the woman always gave off super-bitch vibes. Raya had tried to stay clear of her husband's boss.

There were times she would admit she was scared of the woman.

"Well, we'll just have to keep you around so you can hear it more."

CHAPTER 4

The food and wine were marvelous. Raya was never one to shy away from eating.

Food comforted her, and when it was as delicious as what she just ate, she didn't even feel bad about leaving her plate empty.

"Oh, my. Sue outdid herself." Raya reached for her wine and took a sip. The Chianti was a very dry, red wine. Though she leaned toward a decent glass of white wine, tonight, Hadley had chosen. The cherry aroma hit her nose when she inhaled.

"I'm glad you liked it. This is one of my favorite meals."

"Well, you certainly have good taste." Raya held her almost empty glass up to salute Hadley.

They had enjoyed their meal in the formal dining room at a table that could easily seat twenty people.

"That, I do." Hadley tipped back her glass and finished off her wine.

Raya smiled and finished hers off as well, the tart flavor coating her tongue. She closed her eyes, enjoying the flavor and wanting another glass.

She glanced up to find Hadley leaning back in her chair, her gaze locked on hers. The entire dinner, their conversation flowed with ease. It was as if Raya could almost forget she was bound to Hadley by a contract.

Candles burned bright on the table, providing the only light in the room. But now, Raya didn't have anything else to occupy herself.

Her food was gone, as was her wine.

"Come here, Raya," Hadley beckoned, her voice sending an electric bolt straight to Raya's core. Pure desire spiraled inside of her, unlike anything she'd ever felt before.

Moisture gathered at the apex of her thighs.

All Raya knew was that she wanted Hadley.

It was wrong, she knew. But there was something about the woman and her intense stare that aroused Raya.

Her first thought was to use the word that was to be removed from her vocabulary.

But somehow, she found herself standing from her seat instead.

Her heels clicked across the marble floor, her hips swaying seductively.

Hadley pushed back from the table and continued to watch her, like a hunter stalking her prey.

"Remove the robe," Hadley ordered.

Raya did as she was told, letting it flutter to the floor somewhere behind her. She arrived at Hadley's side, dressed in the negligee and heels only.

"Yes?" Raya bit her lip to keep from moaning.

How the hell was she this turned on by just a look? She'd never had this reaction to her husband.

"You're so fucking beautiful." Standing, she cupped Raya's jaw and smashed her lips to hers.

Raya had been waiting for this moment.

And it was so good.

When Hadley's tongue stroked hers, Raya moaned.

She needed more.

Raya pressed closer to Hadley, who guided her toward the table.

Before Raya knew it, she was propped up onto the table, neither of them breaking the kiss.

They ignored the sound of dishes crashing to the floor.

Hadley deepened the kiss while her hands began exploring Raya's body.

The sound of material ripping filled the air, causing Raya to gasp.

"I knew I purchased this for a reason," Hadley muttered, her eyes roaming Raya's now naked body with a hunger that took Raya's breath away.

She bent her head down and captured Raya's tit with her lips, taking her time bathing it with her tongue.

Raya groaned, her fingers diving into Hadley's thick hair. Her pussy grew slicker as Hadley continued to suckle her mound.

"God, your skin is so soft," Hadley said as she lifted her head and claimed Raya's lips again. Raya drew Hadley between her legs, needing her closer.

Hadley's kisses were becoming addictive.

Raya cried out when Hadley trailed hot kisses along her jawline and down her shoulder, until she was able to capture the other breast.

Pleasure spread throughout her body as the billionaire took her time worshipping her breast.

"I want my dessert now. Lay back and open those pretty thighs of yours."

She did as she was commanded, knocking more of the dishes off and onto the floor. If Hadley didn't care, neither did she. She was sure the woman could afford new plates and glasses, after all.

Guiding her ass to the edge of the table, Hadley ordered, "Wider." Raya didn't hesitate, her cunt dripping with wetness. "This pussy now belongs to me." Raya cried out and jerked when Hadley rolled her clit between her fingers. "Hold still or you'll fall."

Raya squeezed her eyes shut, basking in the sensations coursing through her body, and soon found herself moaning Hadley's name. She didn't care how loud she was, or if anyone in the house could hear her.

"Look at how fucking wet you are." Sliding her hands underneath Raya's ass, she leaned down and started devouring her.

The woman certainly knew how to eat pussy. She licked and sucked until Raya was practically begging her to climax.

"Hadley!" Raya cried out, her fingers digging into Hadley's thick blonde hair as she continued to suckle her clit.

She was so good at this. Her tongue touched every inch of Raya's pussy, always returning to her clit.

It had taken Brandon a while until he learned how to make her climax while he ate her out, and here Hadley was, about to make her cum within a second of her tongue touching her.

Raya's back arched off the table in ecstasy. Another lick, Raya detonated.

Her scream filled the air. Her body shook as pleasure raced through her before slumping back down onto the table.

This was hands down the fastest she'd ever reached completion.

"Just as sweet as I knew you would be."

Raya opened her eyes to find Hadley watching her. The woman ran a hand along Raya's thigh while licking her lips.

"Wow."

It was all Raya could say, her body still tingling from the powerful climax.

"This body of yours is to be cherished, pleasured," Hadley began, making Raya's stomach quiver as she brushed her fingers along her skin. "I want to give you all the pleasure in the world, to spoil you…to make you mine."

Raya gasped at her words.

But her declaration piqued Raya's interest.

Even though her husband stole from her, she wanted to pleasure Raya? Spoil her?

What kind of game was she playing?

"Will you allow me the pleasure to do all of those things?"

Hadley held out her hand, assisting Raya into a sitting position on the table. Raya watched her, unsure of what to say.

"Why?" she asked. Clearing her throat, she continued. "Why would you want to do all that, knowing my husband stole from you?"

A faint smile crossed the billionaire's lips.

"Your husband is an idiot. He doesn't even

realize what he has right in front of him." Cupping Raya's face, she gently rubbed her thumb along her cheek, and Raya found herself leaning into Hadley's warmth. The woman gathered her close, and the gentle embrace tugged at her heartstrings. Affection and tenderness was not something she considered when thinking of Hadley Hamilton before today. "But you…I've always had my eyes on you, and I mean what I say. When has anyone ever focused just on you, Raya? You care for everyone else, including that thief. I want to give you nothing but pleasure."

Raya studied Hadley. From what she'd heard from Brandon, Hadley was a businesswoman, and one of her word.

"Can I?" Hadley asked, her voice breaking into Raya's thoughts.

"Yes."

※

Raya moaned, unsure of the last time she'd had such a vivid sex dream. Her legs were pushed open wide, and her clit was getting the most attention it had received in a long time.

With a smile, she reached down to hold her imaginary lover's head in place. They could just keep on licking her with their magical tongue—

Wait a minute.

Opening her eyes, Raya looked down and found Hadley's head buried between her legs.

"Ohhh," she moaned.

Hadley murmured, "So fucking good," while continuing to lap up her juices.

Waking up to getting head shot up to the top of her list of favorite activities. Brandon always joked about his morning wood, and how it was her wifely duty to handle it, but never did he offer to lick her pussy first thing in the morning.

Raya relaxed her legs more as Hadley focused on her clit, licking and suckling it. Raya raised her hips off the mattress and thrust forward, riding Hadley's wicked tongue.

"Yes," she hissed, the fire burning inside of her growing. She wanted to climax, explode on Hadley's tongue, just as she did last night at dinner.

Hadley was going to ruin her.

Raya's muscles tightened as she crested.

Her throat was going to be raw by the end of the week with these orgasms.

"Hadley!" she cried out before flopping back onto the bed, out of breath. Her clit tingled, and a smile appeared on Raya's face. It was the best feeling.

One where her pussy had been eaten properly.

Hadley climbed over her, resting her hands on each side of her head. Something hard brushed Raya's leg. Glancing down, she took in the strap-on attached to Hadley's body. The thick cock was impressive.

Her core clenched, ready to feel something stretch her out.

Her husband was a decent sized guy, and she hadn't really had any complaints. But the cock attached to Hadley would give any man a run for his money.

Raya parted her lips, just as Hadley's came crashing down on them.

Raya savored every moment of the kiss that grew harder, bolder. She was no longer shy or hesitant, and returned the kiss with the same fervor.

Raya whimpered when Hadley settled between her thighs, the cock brushing against her slick opening.

"Someone wants my cock inside of her," Hadley murmured, raining kisses along Raya's lips, chin, jawline, and neck, scraping her teeth against the sensitive skin.

"Please, fuck me with that big cock," Raya begged, her pussy aching to be filled and stretched.

"How can I say no when you ask to be fucked so nicely?" Hadley lined the blunt tip to Raya's opening, and with one thrust, she sank completely into Raya.

"Ah!" Raya cried out, her pussy trying to accommodate its wide girth. Her pussy burned slightly while Hadley held still to allow her to get used to the invasion.

Fuck.

It was the best feeling in the world. Raya had never felt so full. Wrapping her legs around Hadley, she threw her head back and moaned.

"Look at you, taking this cock." Hadley withdrew, leaving the tip inside before thrusting hard.

Raya rocked her hips to meet Hadley, thrust for thrust.

"God, it feels so good. I'm so full," she groaned. Unable to resist Hadley's breasts swaying in front of her face, she latched onto one.

It was her first time sucking a tit, but she was a quick study. She knew what she liked, so it wasn't going to be hard for her to learn to please a woman.

Hadley groaned, her breaths coming faster as she pushed off the bed, popping her tit from Raya's mouth. Settling on her knees, she rested her hands on the back of Raya's thighs and shifted angles so she could pound deeper into her.

"Yes," Raya cried out.

The woman was utterly fucking her first thing in the morning, and Raya was loving it.

Soon Hadley paused, leaving her fake cock buried inside of Raya while she slid her finger along her pussy, gathering her juices on her fingers.

Raya's pussy clenched around the cock, tremors wracking her body.

Her swollen clit was sensitive, and Hadley was steadily increasing the pressure of her fingers. Her core clenched, gripping the cock while she rode out the waves of ecstasy washing over her.

A scream tore from her throat.

Her orgasm slammed into her like a freight train hitting a brick wall.

Her body arched off the bed as a euphoric sensation came over her. Her senses closed off as she rode the waves of the hard orgasm.

When she finally calmed down, she relaxed on the bed and opened her eyes when Hadley withdrew the cock. Hadley was staring down at her with a pleased expression on her face.

"Good morning, my love."

CHAPTER 5

Every morning, Hadley woke Raya up with an orgasm, and every night she fell asleep after Hadley pulled another one from her.

Raya was addicted to the orgasms Hadley gave her.

She had to admit that when Hadley was gone and at work, she pined for the woman.

She was like a strung-out heroin addict waiting for her next fix.

Only, it was her next climax.

Raya now understood sex addicts.

Hadley fucked her so good every day, she couldn't wait for the next time.

Rolling over in her bed, she glanced at the clock. It was the weekend, and Hadley had already given her morning orgasm, and Raya had fallen back to sleep afterward.

They had settled into a nice routine during the week. Being that it was the weekend, Raya thought Hadley would have remained in the bed with her.

As promised, Hadley had only focused on her pleasure, leaving Raya to feel as if she was a poor lover.

Taking, but never giving.

Every time she'd tried, Hadley brushed her aside, saying that it was all about her.

She pouted.

She wanted to give Hadley pleasure too. She was a giving person, and was determined to get her off.

Standing from the bed, she padded into the bathroom where she quickly handled nature's call. There was no sign of Hadley, so she went ahead and jumped into the shower.

Twenty minutes later, she emerged, feeling like a new woman, her skin scrubbed until it glowed. After detangling her wet hair with a brush, she set out to find Hadley.

Walking toward her closet, she saw the door to the veranda open. Dropping her towel, she snagged one of her silk robes and put it on.

Heading toward the door, she took notice of how her heart raced with the thought of seeing Hadley.

She found her sexy lover sitting at the table with a full spread of food set out before her.

"Good morning," she said, closing the door behind her. Breathing in the fresh air, Raya smiled. The view of the hills and the ocean captivated her every time she came out here. It was her favorite place to go and to write.

Hadley looked beautiful, dressed in a white robe and house slippers, her blonde hair pulled back in a low ponytail.

Her gaze cut to Raya. "You don't need that on."

Raya undid the ties and removed the robe as she made her way to Hadley.

The cold morning air teased her nipples, causing them to bead into tight buds. Hadley's eyes darkened when Raya straddled her lap.

"Good morning," she repeated, offering her lips to the woman she temporarily belonged to.

"Morning." Hadley gathered her close and gave her a slow, deep, passionate kiss, one that soon turned desperate.

Raya's body was going up in flames. Being naked outside at one point would have made her uncomfortable, but now, she didn't care.

They were on private property, and if Hadley wanted her naked, then she'd be naked.

Raya pressed closer to Hadley, not wanting anything to fit in between them. Hadley reached up and cupped Raya's plump mounds in her hands, guiding one to her lips, sucking it deep into her mouth. Raya threw her head back and arched into her.

If this was how they would spend Sundays, then she would be down for it.

"Your body is so damn responsive to me," Hadley mumbled, her lips brushing Raya's nipple. Trailing her tongue along Raya's chest, she captured the other one.

"I don't know what you've done to me, but I like it," Raya joked.

"Just fucked you properly, I guess. Wouldn't you say?" Hadley teased, her hand trailing down Raya's torso to slip between her thighs. Raya already knew what Hadley would find.

A super soaked pussy.

"Christ," Hadley purred, dipping her fingers into Raya's core. "All this honey is for me?"

Raya jerked her head in a nod.

Hadley's fingers slid along her slit until she reached Raya's swollen clit.

Raya gripped the back of the chair, preparing for the ride to pleasure town.

Hadley flicked the swollen bean fast, increasing her speed and pressure.

Raya's hips rotated, riding Hadley's hand.

"Hadley," Raya began to chant, knowing her orgasm was going to be quick and hard.

"I love it when you call my name. I want you to scream it when you cum."

Raya arched her back, again offering her tits to Hadley, who didn't disappoint. Her lips closed around one nipple, and she released a growl.

The sound was so damn sexy to Raya.

Hadley got her request.

"Hadley!" she screamed through her orgasm. Her muscles grew tense, her nails digging into the cushions of the chair as an electrical current spread through her.

Biting her lip, she continued to thrust her hips against Hadley's hand, not wanting the feeling to stop.

"Atta, girl." Reaching up, she guided Raya's face to hers, kissing her deep before pulling away. She brought her fingers up to her lips and licked them clean. "I can't get enough of your juices."

"I can't get enough of you, making me cum the way you do."

Raya grinned and wiggled her naked bottom, vowing they would fuck all day. Her writing was ahead of schedule, and she was pleased with the amount of work she had gotten done during the week.

"You need to eat, and today, pack." Hadley spun her around on her lap and pulled a plate forward for her.

"Pack? Where are we going?" Raya asked. Picking up a fork, Hadley stabbed into the omelet and brought it to her lips.

Sue strikes again.

Can that woman mess up anything?

"Paris."

Raya froze and turned to face her. "Are you

shitting me?"

Hadley offered her one of her rare smiles, one that lit up her face and made her appear younger than her forty-five years.

"Why would I lie? We're going to fly out late tonight so that we'll arrive by tomorrow morning." Her free hand rested on Raya's hip while she stabbed the fork into more food, offering it to Raya.

Paris?

She loved the city of lights.

After she swallowed her food, she reached for the glass of OJ and took a hefty swallow.

"What should I pack?"

"Light. I'll buy you everything you'll need there."

Raya froze.

Shopping in Paris?

Raya turned to Hadley and cupped her face in her hands.

"Thank you," she whispered, her lips brushing across Hadley's. This time, Raya controlled the kiss, which started off soft and slow, but soon deepened.

When they broke apart, they were both breathing heavily.

"You're welcome. Now, let me finish feeding you."

Raya arched an eyebrow at her. "You do know I can feed myself."

"Of course, but I want to do it." Once more, Hadley picked at the food and raised the fork to her lips. Giving in, she accepted the bite and chewed, the flavors bursting on her tongue. "And after you eat, there's something you need to do."

Raya frowned.

What did she have to do on a Sunday?

Swallowing, she wiped her mouth with the napkin. "What is that?"

"You need to call Brandon. It's almost noon."

※

Lying across her bed, Raya stared at her cellphone. How had she forgotten Sunday was the day she was to speak with her husband?

Sundays at noon was the agreement.

She didn't know whether she should do a FaceTime call or an old-fashion audio one.

"Let's just get this over with." She chose

FaceTime. Having replaced her robe, she sat up on the bed and hit the button for Brandon's number.

After the second ring, his face came onto the screen.

"Raya," he breathed.

She offered him a tight smile. His hair was standing on end, as if he had been running his hands through it.

"How are you?" she asked.

"I should be asking you that, baby. You are always worried about me." His face relaxed, a small smile playing on his lips. "You look good. Is Hadley treating you well?"

Raya chewed on her lip, thinking of how well Hadley had been treating her. She had to fight down the warmth spreading through her cheeks, praying he didn't notice it.

Hadley was taking damn good care of her.

"She is. Her house is lovely, and I've been getting a lot of writing done."

"That's good, baby. I've lined up a few interviews. I'm going to get back on my feet." She took in the background, and noticed he was sitting on the couch in their family room. What she should have seen was the home they had built together with their hard work.

But the image was ruined by the thought of it being stolen.

"That's great, Brandon," she sniffed, holding back a retort. Had he just done his job at Hamilton Technologies and not embezzled, he wouldn't be out of a job. But then, she wouldn't be a guest of Hadley's.

Her heart skipped a beat at the thought of the billionaire.

"I'm going to make all of this right, I promise."

She nodded. It was a shame that after all the time they had together, she was having doubts about her own husband.

He had broken the trust she had had in him. Never would she had thought he would have done something like that.

What if Hadley would have notified the authorities? Something like this would have hit the media, and could have ruined her as well. She wrote under her real name, and news of her husband's thievery could have harmed her business.

He hadn't thought of her.

"Okay," she whispered, tucking her dark hair behind her ear.

DON'T TELL ME NO

"You don't look too happy to see me. Are you okay?"

She met his gaze. Did he really want to know what she was thinking?

"Newsflash, dear husband," she snapped, angry with how his actions had affected her. She was basically the property of a rich woman because he had stolen from her, and she was the debt that must be paid. "You stole from a powerful woman who demanded you sign your wife over to her to repay the millions you stole. Why did you even need to steal? We make great money, lived a great life. We didn't want for anything, and you became greedy."

Since finding out what he had done, she had been going through the motions and barely able to comprehend everything. Her first thought was: how could she protect her husband? How could she help him through this? Keep him out of jail?

If he had just taken a moment to think of how his deception would affect her—but he never thought of her.

Always making decisions first, sharing them with her later.

In the past, she hadn't minded. She

thought it was cute, and just Brandon's way of taking care of her.

"Just calm down, baby. I'm trying to make this right," he proclaimed, exasperated.

"Are you?" she snarled, brushing her hair from her face. "What could you possibly do to make this better? I signed a contract to keep you out of jail. Six months I'm to be here."

"I'm going to meet with Hadley and offer to pay the money back—"

"We don't have millions just sitting aside somewhere, Brandon." They had a nice amount in all of their accounts, and paying Hadley back would take everything they had. She ran a hand along her face before focusing on the phone again.

"Trust me, Raya. I'm going to make this right."

Tears blurred her vision. Blinking them back, she blew out a deep breath.

"I have to go. I need to pack."

His brows furrowed. "Where are you going?"

"Hadley needs to go to Paris for a business meeting, and I'm to go with her."

"Why?"

"Because I signed a fucking contract that

says I have to go anywhere, whenever she wants me to. Remember the one word I can't utter?"

"Okay, okay, calm down." She narrowed her gaze, knowing that if she were standing in front of him right now, her hands would be wrapped around his neck. "How long are you going to be in Paris?"

"I'm not sure. A week?"

"I'm sure you will have fun in Paris." A look of worry briefly crossed his face, but then it was gone. "I love you so much, Raya. I can't wait to hold you in my arms again."

Raya paused. "I love you too, Brandon."

She hit the red button on her phone to disconnect the call. She was faced with a heavy feeling settling in her chest.

Did she still love Brandon?

CHAPTER 6

"Beautiful, isn't it?" Hadley murmured. Raya turned from where she stood on the balcony of their suite. The luxury hotel faced the Eiffel Tower, giving her a front-row seat of the beautiful light display.

Darkness had fallen on the beautiful city. They had arrived that morning, and had spent the day sightseeing, shopping, and dining at the finest restaurants.

Raya turned to Hadley, who held two glasses of wine in her hand. "I think standing here gazing onto the tower is my favorite part of the day."

She accepted the offered wine and took a sip. Of course, it was delicious. Hadley had exquisite taste, and Raya had yet to be disappointed by any of the choices in food, wine, or clothes that Hadley had made.

Her attention was drawn back to the magical display.

Hadley wrapped her arm around Raya's waist and brought her close, their bodies always molding together so perfectly.

"Tonight, we are going to visit with some old friends of mine."

"Really?" Raya blinked, turning in Hadley's arms.

"Yes. There is a club I want to take you to. One that is unlike anything I'm sure you've ever been to before." Reaching up, she brushed Raya's hair from her face, her soft caress sending a chill down her spine.

"I'm sure it will be fun." Raya offered her a smile. She wasn't sure what kind of club Hadley was hinting at, but she knew she couldn't refuse.

After spending so much time with Hadley, she wasn't sure she wanted to say no. Something in her eyes piqued her own curiosity.

Hadley's hand slid down the curve of Raya's back and cupped her ass.

"It's a private club I've been a member of for some years. Very exclusive." She gave Raya a squeeze and kissed her. "I already have your outfit laid out on the bed for you."

She was getting used to Hadley's spoiling. Every store they entered, she walked out with a few bags.

She'd had a blast, and couldn't remember the last time she had done so much shopping just for herself.

Tossing back the rest of her wine, she spun on her heel and raced into the suite, giggling at the sight of a white box with a red bow sitting on the bed.

Their presidential suite was located on the top floor of the hotel, dripping with luxury.

Priceless crystal chandeliers, two wood-burning fireplaces, a living room, dining room, three bedrooms, and four full baths.

Raya had never stayed in such a suite.

Setting down her empty glass on the nightstand, she reached for the box and untied the red bow. Hadley's heels echoed against the marble floor as she sauntered into the room, her lips curved up into a sexy smile as she watched Raya.

Pulling the top off the box, she dropped it on the bed before moving the soft, white gift paper out of the way. She gasped as her gaze settled on the items nestled inside the box.

"Oh, my," she gushed. A sexy black lace bra with a golden clasp and matching thong held her attention. "It's beautiful, but this is all I'm to wear?"

Coming to stand behind Raya, she brushed her dark hair to the side and kissed her neck. "Yes. You are going to make everyone jealous. I have one more gift for you."

Raya moved to spin around, but Hadley's hand stopped her.

"Wait." Setting her glass down next to Raya's, she opened the drawer.

Raya's heart raced. What woman wouldn't get excited about receiving gifts?

"Lift your hair up." Doing as she was told, Hadley reached around and placed something along her throat. The coolness made Raya shiver. She only caught a glimpse of the diamonds, and she was sure they weren't cubic zirconia. Hadley finished with the clasp and stepped back. "Done. Go look in the mirror."

Dashing over to the mirror on the wall, she froze. Her hand immediately lifted to trace the beautiful diamond and gold pendant choker that surrounded her neck. On the gold pendant were two H's.

No doubt, Hadley's initials.

Hadley wrapped her arms around her.

"Like it?"

"Oh, my goodness. It's so beautiful…and so expensive." The diamonds were beautiful, and the way the light flashed across them left Raya speechless. "I can't take this."

It was one thing to accept clothing, but jewelry that was no doubt worth six figures was another thing.

"It is my gift to you. This will allow everyone in the club to know you belong to me." Hadley's voice grew low, her hands sliding along Raya's torso and up to her breasts. "I want everyone to know that you belong to me. The choker was worth every penny. This body was made to be cherished and fucked."

Raya's neck rolled back and rested on Hadley's shoulder, her body responding to Hadley as it always did. Her core clenched with need as Hadley pinched her breasts.

"Hadley," she groaned.

"You deserve to have nothing but the best. These diamonds pale in comparison to your beauty," Hadley claimed, her lips brushing against Raya's sensitive skin. "I want to give you everything you have ever desired, Raya. Tonight will be all about you."

※

Raya sat in the back of the dark limo, her heart racing erratically. She was dressed in only the bra, thong, black Louboutin heels, and her diamond choker. A dark trench coat completed her outfit to protect her from prying eyes when leaving the hotel.

Hadley was dressed in dark slacks, a blouse, and heels. Her blonde hair was left down, and the bright red color on her lips highlighted them perfectly.

Going into the unknown had Raya slightly turned on. She quickly figured they must be going to a sex club of some sort. It would be the only reason Hadley would allow her to wear such an outfit.

The car drew to a halt, and within seconds, the door was opened by a valet.

"Good evening, Ms. Hamilton." The man reached out a hand and guided Hadley out of the car. Turning back to Raya, he assisted her out as well. "Mrs. White."

She was unsure how he knew her name, but she let it go, focusing on the unmarked building. A few people lingered around the entrance, apparently waiting on the valet to bring their vehicles.

"Come, my love." Holding her arm for Raya, she slipped hers around Hadley's and allowed her to draw her in close. They walked up the few stairs to the door where a woman dressed in a uniform greeted them with a wide grin.

"Good evening, ladies," she greeted with a heavy French accent as she opened the large wooden door.

"Hello, Kelly." Hadley smiled at her and guided Raya inside, leading her down a short hallway that led to the central area.

The interior of the club was dark, with a few strobe lights highlighting the area. The atmosphere was electric, causing the hairs on the back of Raya's neck to stand up. Music flowed through invisible speakers. The bar was highlighted with pink neon lights.

Raya was right.

It was a sex club. And from the looks of it, a lesbian one.

Raya scanned the club and found women in all stages of dress. Her gaze landed on a couple lying on a chaise, openly having sex with an audience surrounding them.

Her confidence wavered. She didn't know if she could walk around as proudly as some of the women here.

"May I take your coats?" a soft voice asked. Raya turned to find a petite Asian woman dressed in the same uniform as the woman at the door, patiently waiting with a small smile on her lips.

Raya's heart pounded as she played with the ties of her coat.

She turned her attention to Hadley, who gave her a quick nod. Swallowing hard, she undid the ties and allowed the woman to assist with removing her coat. Cold air fluttered along Raya's skin. Her nipples tightened, and her stomach quivered.

"Thank you," Raya murmured before turning back to Hadley, who held her hand out. The heat radiating from Hadley's eyes made Raya pause.

Standing tall, she pushed down the small shred of doubt and took Hadley's hand.

Bringing it up to her lips, and pressed a kiss to the back.

"Beautiful," Hadley praised, her heated gaze dropping down to Raya's stiff nipples on full display. "Come. Let's go find my friends."

Raya walked along with a more pronounced sway to her lips as Hadley guided her through the establishment, stopping at a table where a few businesswomen sat.

"Hadley, who is your friend?" A tall, gorgeous brunette stood from the table, her hungry gaze roaming over Raya's body.

"Hello, Janet. This is my Raya." Lifting their arms in the air, Hadley twirled Raya around so that her friends could take her. Hadley brought Raya flush to her side and motioned her hand around the table. "Raya, these are my friends: Janet, Maria, Caitlyn, and Victoria."

Raya offered them a small smile. "So nice to meet you." The four women didn't hide their assessment of her, or the lust in their eyes, mixed with a hint of jealousy.

"The pleasure is all ours, my dear." Janet boldly moved around Raya and stopped on her other side. "If Hadley allows you, I would love to get to play with you."

Raya's gaze flew to Janet in shock. She spoke as if Hadley wasn't standing next to her.

"We'll see, Janet," Hadley rested a hand along the small of Raya's back. "This is her first night in the club. I wanted to get her feet a little wet tonight."

"There's something I wouldn't mind helping to make wet," Marie snorted, causing the others to chuckle.

Raya's cheeks heated. Given the chance, these women would spread her out on their table and devour her like an open buffet.

"We're going to look around a little. Save us a seat, will you?" Hadley asked.

"Of course. We would love to get to know your Raya." Caitlyn tossed her a wink. "We may move over to our usual spot. There are too many people here tonight."

They went farther into the club, where the scene changed. There were different rooms with all sorts of sexual activities going on. Raya tried to not walk around with her mouth on the ground.

The club was filled with women who loved women.

There was a room with a crowd watching a woman who was tied up, receiving her punishment. Raya had to fight to keep from cringing. Pain wasn't something she was into.

After the third room, Raya was no longer shocked by what she saw.

They arrived at a room encased in glass, the square enclosure surrounded by an audience. Hadley led Raya over, where in the center of the room was an oversized chaise with a few plush chairs scattered around the small enclosure. Two women were currently the center of attention. Naked, they stood by one of the walls. The dark-haired one suddenly pushed the short red-haired woman against the glass.

Murmurs echoed through the air.

Raya watched with bated breath as she leaned into the woman, kissing her. Their moans could be heard from small speakers posted along the walls.

Raya stepped closer to the glass, captivated by the two. They didn't care about the crowd watching them. Her core clenched, watching the dark-haired one bend down and take the other's tit into her mouth.

"Like what you see in there?"

Raya glanced at Hadley before turning back to the scene unfolding before her and nodded. Hadley nuzzled her neck. "Want to go in there?"

Raya stiffened.

"I...um..."

Turning Raya around, Hadley covered her mouth with hers. "I promise, you will like it." Hadley dominated the kiss, holding Raya's face in her hands, literally taking her breath away. "I told you, this body was made for pleasure, and meant to be cherished. Tonight, they will take care of you. Those women saw you and wanted you. They are jealous of me that I get to have you."

She had to admit, her secret fantasy was of having someone watch her. There were times she would masturbate with her vibrator, imagining someone getting off while watching her.

Had she ever shared that with her husband?

Hell no.

He wouldn't have understood.

Looking at the couple through the glass walls, she made up her mind.

"Come in with me?" Raya asked.

"Of course." Hadley pressed a hard kiss to Raya's lips and took her hand before opening the door, motioning for Raya to enter.

Letting out a deep breath, Raya walked into the glass room.

CHAPTER 7

"Ladies," Hadley's husky voice called out. The two women paused what they were doing and glanced at Hadley. "Shelby. Angie."

Raya held onto Hadley's hand while her heart tried to pound its way out of her chest. It was no surprise that Hadley would know the women's names. It would appear she was a frequent attendee of the establishment; everyone seemed to know her. Hadley had been drawing attention from the moment they entered the club.

Raya was secretly growing jealous.

Hadley was hers.

"Look who it is, Angie." Shelby, the dark-haired one, murmured, pointing to Hadley. "She's brought us someone to play with."

"Hadley, who's your sexy toy?" Angie gave a throaty laugh as she slid her hand along Shelby's hip, licking her lips.

"This is my Raya. This is her first time here." Hadley brought Raya forward. She stepped behind her to present her to not only the women in the room, but the ones watching as well. "She means something to me, and I want to make sure she feels good when we leave tonight."

Raya's heart skipped a beat at Hadley's words.

She means something to me.

Shelby smiled. "She's beautiful." Taking Angie's hand, they walked over to Raya, their eyes roaming her body. Raya took the time to look at them too. Both were in great shape, with high breasts and firm, round hips.

The complete opposite of her thick and curvy physique.

Raya grew excited. Her nipples beaded, and her core was already growing slick. Two women were going to take her with an audience? She swallowed hard at the anticipating growing inside of her.

"You know you don't have to worry about a thing. We'll take excellent care of Raya."

Angie reached up and trailed a finger along Raya's bare shoulder.

"Look at these tits," Shelby purred, trailing a finger around Raya's protruding nipple. "I can't wait to taste them."

"Have fun," Hadley whispered in Raya's ear, pressing a kiss to the side of her neck before stepping away. Raya watched her take a seat, a small smile playing on her lips.

Shelby and Angie surrounded her, their hands caressing her skin as they pressed up against her.

"We'll be gentle," Angie promised, stroking Raya's hair. Her hand slipped down to the clasp nestled between Raya's breasts and opened it, while Shelby helped push her panties down.

Shelby leaned in, nuzzling her face into the crook of Raya's neck, the lace material that had once covered her breasts slipping to the floor.

Tremors snuck through her as she grew more aroused.

Two sets of hands on her.

Two sets of lips.

Countless amounts of eyes on her.

All that really mattered was that Hadley was watching.

Fingers dove into her hair and yanked her head back, causing her to gasp.

Shelby smothered it by slipping her tongue inside Raya's mouth, all while Angie cradled and massaged Raya's plump mounds before traveling down to her stomach.

Raya reached up and held Shelby's head, deepening their kiss. A throaty groan escaped her as Angie's fingers parted Raya's folds, connecting with Raya's swollen clit.

Shelby tore her mouth from Raya's and tipped her face toward Angie's. Their lips met in a hot, sizzling kiss.

Raya's hips thrust forward against Angie's hand, who continued to strum Raya's sensitive bean while Shelby teased and played with Raya's tits.

"The chaise," Shelby gasped.

Raya opened her eyes once Angie disconnected their lips, and watched Angie lick her fingers clean.

Angie chuckled. "Hurry. I need to taste Raya."

Shelby took Raya by the hand and led her over to the plush chaise, big enough to fit two people on it. They assisted Raya down onto it, the smooth velvet soft as it slid across her skin.

Raya's pussy was slick and aching. Her gaze roamed the glass room, finding a larger crowd watching. She caught sight of a few of Hadley's friends standing outside the room.

"Get comfy, honey." Angie winked, guiding Raya's legs open as she settled herself at her core.

Shelby immediately latched onto Raya's breast, licking and sucking.

Arching her back, Raya turned her head to find Hadley. Their eyes connected, and she could see the heat blazing in her stare as she cried out when Angie's mouth covered her pussy.

While Angie and Shelby worked her body, Raya couldn't look away from Hadley. She wanted to make sure the billionaire saw how much she liked having two women attend to her.

Angie sucked and pulled on her clit.

"Hadley!" Raya cried out, riding Angie's tongue. It didn't matter who was eating her out; it was Hadley's name that ripped through her lips.

Raya threw her head back in ecstasy, living out her fantasy on steroids. Pleasure coursed through her body as the two women continued to work her over. Pushing two fingers inside of her, Angie began pumping in and out as she suckled Raya's clit.

Her eyes flew open, and she was met with the hot stares of those watching.

Seeing them engaging with each other while watching her receive pleasure sent her skyrocketing to the heavens.

Her orgasm crashed into her, forcing her back to arch off the couch. Angie was relentless with that tongue of hers.

Finally, she flopped back down, her body covered in a fine coating of sweat. Her chest rose and fell rapidly as she tried to catch her breath.

"Oh, my," she whispered.

Shelby giggled. "That was sexy as hell."

Angie gave Raya's pussy one long lick before raising her head up, her mouth shiny with Raya's juices.

"So sweet. So good," she murmured, pressing a kiss to Raya's thigh.

Raya's attention was captured by the sight

of Hadley walking toward them with nothing on but her thick strap-on.

Raya swallowed hard.

She hadn't realized that Hadley had it with her.

"Move over, girls. My turn," Hadley declared.

Angie scurried to the other side of the chaise as Hadley knelt down beside Raya, stroking the thick cock, her intense stare locked on Raya.

"Hadley," Raya murmured, unable to tear her gaze from the sexy blonde.

"You are so fucking beautiful, Raya. I loved seeing Shelby and Angie bring you pleasure." Hadley reached out and slipped her fingers into Raya's slick slit, and then brought her fingers to her lips. "Always so sweet. I love the taste of your pussy."

Angie and Shelby began to suckle on her breasts. Her body was overly sensitive after such an intense climax.

"You like being fucked in front of all these women?" Hadley asked, waving a hand toward the glass walls.

"Yes," she answered quietly.

"I can't hear you, Raya. Speak up. They

want to hear your answer, just as I do." Snapping her fingers, Shelby and Angie reached down and lifted Raya's legs into the air.

"Yes!" Raya hollered, not caring who was watching them. She just wanted to feel the thick, fake cock breach her slick pussy.

Hadley thrust forward, sinking it deep inside of her. She cried out from the invasion, her pussy stretching to accommodate the wide girth. There was some pain, but it quickly dissipated.

Hadley remained on her knees, pounding into Raya, who writhed on the chaise while the three women attended to her every need.

There were hands and lips everywhere as Hadley continued to fuck her hard. Her body trembled from the amount of pleasure racing through her body.

Her hands reached out, trying to find something to hold onto, which was Shelby and Angie's heads. Her fingers threaded through their hair, using them as her anchor. Angie moved higher and claimed Raya's lips.

The faint hint of her own pussy greeted her.

Fingers began to rub her clit while

Hadley's strokes grew deeper. Her legs were brought back farther, opening her even more.

Raya tore her lips from Angie's and screamed, "Ahhh!" Hadley moved faster, sending the cock deeper. Raya couldn't take any more.

Her muscles tightened, and her orgasm claimed her.

"Hadley!" Her cry pierced the air. Tears escaped her eyes as her climax took over her body. Tremors shook her while her release poured from her. She fell back against the chaise, completely spent.

Angie and Shelby released her legs. Without opening her eyes, she felt Hadley lean over her, tracing her fingers along her face.

"Open your eyes, love."

Raya did as she was told, and met Hadley's eyes. Her lover rested her body on top of Raya, her fake cock still buried inside of her. Raya hooked her ankles together behind Hadley, entrapping her on top of her, their breasts crushed between them.

Hadley claimed her lips in a soft kiss. As always, she dominated the kiss, slowly stroking Raya's tongue with hers.

It was as if it was only the two of them, everyone around them was forgotten.

Raya moaned, lifting her arms up and wrapping them around Hadley, getting lost in the kiss. After climaxing twice, she was sure her juices were all over her, Hadley, and the couch, but Raya couldn't care less.

At that moment, she loved where she was, and didn't give a damn about anything else.

※

Hadley entwined her fingers with Raya's as she led her through the club. This time, Raya held her head high with a confidence unbeknownst to her. When they left the glass room, Raya had chosen to remain naked, except for her diamond choker and heels. Hadley had sort of dressed, though her shirt remained unbuttoned. She'd put her pants back on, and carried Raya's bra and thong in her hand.

Eyes followed them as they moved together, yet Raya didn't feel the need to shy away from any appreciative glances.

She felt beautiful.

Sexy.

Desired.

Hadley took them to a private area where Janet, Maria, Caitlyn, and Victoria were seated. Wide plush chairs surrounded a low table that had a fire feature in the center.

Taking a seat, Hadley guided Raya down onto her lap. A server immediately arrived with the finest of wines.

"Having fun?" Caitlyn asked with raised eyebrows. She had been one of the women standing outside the glass walls. Through her lust-filled haze, Raya remembered Caitlyn watching her while another woman knelt on the floor before her, licking her pussy.

"Yes, I am," Raya replied. Hadley wrapped a possessive arm around her waist and brought her back against her.

"I'd say you are. That scene in the glass room was so fucking hot," Maria chuckled, reaching down to snag her glass of wine. "I didn't know if I needed a stiff drink or a cigarette after watching you four in that damn room."

"I told you they would be jealous," Hadley whispered in Raya's ear. Raya bit back a smile, happy that Hadley was pleased with this news. Turning back to the group, she found Janet staring at her. Raya gave her a small smile before turning back to the conversation going on around the table.

"How long are you going to be in Paris, Hadley?" Victoria asked. She waved a female down, who immediately came and sat at her feet. The woman was petite with long, thick brown hair. Her eyes were wide, and her face was young. Raya wasn't going to judge at all on how young the girl looked, but it would be a stretch to say the girl was eighteen.

Hadley's hand slid down Raya's stomach. "We'll probably be here a week. I'm going to take some much needed vacation time and spoil Raya."

Her breath caught in her throat, feeling Hadley's hand continue to move. Her legs instantly opened for her lover. After everything they had done in the glass room, Raya no longer cared who was around them.

"You should take the train to Amsterdam. She would love it," Maria suggested.

Hadley's fingers parted her folds, exposing her clit. Raya leaned back, arching her chest out as she began to rub her.

"Can I taste her?" Janet blurted out.

Hadley chuckled. "Of course, my friend.

Her pussy is one of the sweetest I've ever had."

Janet stood from her chair and knelt down on the floor before them. Hadley spread her legs wide, allowing Raya to do the same as she opened Raya's folds, presenting her clit to Janet.

Raya turned her face toward Hadley's, offering her lips to her. She wasn't even going to question or try to resist. What seemed like a long time ago, Raya had signed a contract, promising to never use the word *no*. After spending so much time with Hadley, she hadn't found one situation where she even wanted to use the word. Hadley claimed her mouth in a brutal kiss, the conversation forgotten.

Janet's warm mouth covered her pussy, taking one long lick of Raya's pussy.

"So good," she muttered, latching onto Raya's clit.

Raya's moan was captured by Hadley's mouth, her tongue pushing inside. Her hands slid up to cup Raya's tits while Janet continued feasting on her.

"Fuck. Tia, baby, come lick Mommy's pussy," Victoria ordered. "Hadley's toy has my pussy so fucking wet. I need to cum."

"Yes, Mommy," Tia replied.

Raya turned herself over to the pleasure that Hadley wanted her to have. Who was she to turn away such attention?

CHAPTER 8

A month had passed since they had returned from Paris. Since then, Raya had moved into Hadley's bedroom. It didn't make sense for them to use two bedrooms.

The weeks flew by, and every Sunday, Raya dreaded her call with Brandon. Every week, he promised to fix things, but now, she didn't know if she wanted that.

Listening to him was like hearing a broken record play on repeat.

Hadley took care of all her needs, wants, and desires. There was nothing left to wish for. Anything Raya wanted, Hadley ensured she got it.

Not that she was materialistic or money-hungry.

No.

When Raya was sad and wanted to watch one of her favorite ugly cry movies, Hadley made sure she did, even watching it with her in the theatre room in the basement.

No matter how small, Hadley went out of her way to make sure she had it.

How had she ever thought Hadley was a monster? But then she realized her perception of the woman was from what Brandon had relayed to her.

Those flirty moments before were just that—Hadley flirting with a married woman.

She had really gotten to know her beyond the hard businesswoman. She had grown up wealthy, but was made to work hard for everything she had. Being a woman in a predominately male world was tough on Hadley, but she was a tough cookie. She grew her company into what it was today.

Typing out a command, her computer froze. "Ugh!" Raya growled. Her five-year-old computer would be considered ancient technology today. The internet was slow, and sometimes she thought she could run down to the library to research what she needed before her computer could. She had spent the better part of the morning in her favorite spot on the veranda, writing. She was almost done with the book she had started on when she first moved into Hadley's mansion.

Picking up her cell, she placed a FaceTime call to Hadley. She knew it was midmorning, but she wanted to see her lover.

Untying her robe, she let it fall to the chair so she was naked from the waist up, something that always pleased Hadley.

"Raya, how are you, my darling?" At the sight of Hadley's beautiful face, Raya smiled brightly, ensuring she caught sight of her perky tits.

"I'm doing well now that I see you," Raya responded. Their relationship had grown leaps and bounds, and Hadley had helped Raya with her sexual awakening. There were even feelings for the woman that Raya hadn't been able to sort out yet. She just knew for the moment, she didn't want to part from the billionaire.

Raya was finally able to convince Hadley to learn to please her. She also had to use all of her skills as a writer to find a loophole to the word *no*.

"*I want to give you pleasure,*" Raya pouted,

leaning into Hadley's embrace as they soaked in the oversized jacuzzi tub in the master bathroom. Hadley squeezed Raya before pressing a kiss to her neck.

"Giving you pleasure and anything you want is enough for me," Hadley murmured.

Raya spun around in the tub and straddled her, bringing them face-to-face.

"But one thing that would give me pleasure is knowing I can give you the same intense orgasms you give me." Raya pressed close, not above using her tits to get what she wanted. Hadley's hands disappeared underneath the water and cupped her ass to hold her close.

Hadley's perfectly sculpted eyebrow rose. "Is that so?"

"I want to learn what things you like, what makes you moan, what makes you scream." Pressing a kiss to Hadley's lips, she tightened her arms around her neck, meaning every word. Hadley had made it her mission to discover everything there was to know about Raya; it would only be fair. Raya wasn't used to anyone taking such good care of her, and she wanted to return the favor. "I want to make you tremble and fall apart."

Hadley brought Raya's head close and covered her mouth with hers. Their kiss was slow, sensual, and erotic. Hadley nipped Raya's bottom lip while her hands traced Raya's back.

"Well, when you ask like that... You know I can't resist you," Hadley admitted. "Come on, baby. Let's get you to bed so you can lick my pussy."

Raya practically spent practically the entire night with her face buried in between Hadley's thighs. It was one of the most magical nights she'd ever experienced.

Raya blinked, coming out of her thoughts.

"Looking at you now makes me want to cancel all my meetings for the day and come home to you."

Raya clenched her legs together, feeling the tingling sensation she always got whenever Hadley gave her that smoldering look.

"I can always come to you," Raya suggested, chewing on her lip, unsure if Hadley would want her to come to her.

"Would you want to come here?"

"If you want me, I'll come to you."

Hadley's voice went low and husky. It was so damn sexy, it sent chills down Raya's spine. "I'll always want you."

Stopping in for a little afternoon loving in the office sounded exciting to Raya. Plus, it would get her out of the house.

They had another trip planned, one that Raya was excited for. They were flying to China for a few meetings and conferences Hadley had to attend. Raya had never been, and she couldn't wait to spend a whole week there.

Since returning from Paris, Raya had flown with Hadley around the U.S., but this would be the first time they left the country.

"Well, then, it looks like I'll be on my way," Raya purred.

"Come just as you are," Hadley growled low.

"Yes, ma'am."

She leaned back in her oversized leather chair. "What did you call for? Did you need something?" Hadley inquired. "I was going to ask if I could use your computer in the office."

"What's wrong with yours?"

"It's old and running slow. I need to do some research, and I'd like to get the information today."

"You can always use the computer in the home office there. You don't even have to ask." She leaned forward. "I'm sending the car to you now. Henry should be there in fifteen minutes."

"See you shortly." Raya blew her a kiss and disconnected the call.

Pushing up from her seat, she gathered her items. She went into their bedroom and put her stuff away before heading toward her closet, needing something to wear so she could appear decent. As much as Hadley loved her naked, she doubted the police would be understanding if she strolled through the streets with no clothes on.

※

Raya sat in the back seat of the luxury sedan that Hadley had sent for her. Henry had been on time, just as Hadley said he would.

Raya teased the waist ties of her jacket. She had chosen a bone-colored, smooth wool wrap coat that had an exaggerated shawl collar that wrapped around her, hiding the fact that she was naked underneath. With long sleeves and a tie-waist belt, it was perfect.

Her only accessories were her diamond

collar, a pair of red Jimmy Choo pumps, and her purse, which she'd stuffed with a few select items. She had pulled her hair up into a messy bun, and for fun, had thrown on some light make-up.

She wanted to look her best when visiting her lover at work.

"We are here, Mrs. White," Henry called out, pulling up in front of the building. A gentleman in a dark valet suit appeared at her door, opened it, and held out his hand.

"Mrs. White. Ms. Hamilton informed me you would be arriving." He offered her a wide smile as he assisted her from the vehicle.

"Thank you." She looked up at the skyscraper that held the Hamilton name on it in bold letters. Memories of the last time she'd arrived at the building came forth. Though this time, there was no dread, only excitement.

It was funny how things changed in such a short period of time.

"Would you like me to escort you to Ms. Hamilton's office?" The young man asked, coming to stand beside her.

She smiled. "No, but thank you. I know where I'm going." Hefting her purse over her shoulder, she sauntered into the building. Unlike last time, the place was bustling with people trying to get on with their day. Raya walked over to the elevator bank and pressed the button. Clasping her hands in front of her, she waited patiently for the car to arrive.

A young businessman came to stand beside her. When she glanced over at him, she found him staring at her. She grinned before turning her attention back to the elevators.

One of the cars arrived.

The man entered after her, hitting the twenty-fourth floor while she hit the thirtieth. He turned to her with a wide smile.

"Important business meeting?" he asked.

"You could say that," she replied, eyeing him warily. He looked vaguely familiar, but she couldn't place him. She stared straight ahead, hoping he recognized the cold shoulder she was giving him.

"If you're going to the thirtieth floor, then it has to be. Hadley Hamilton's office is on that floor. She owns this building." He straightened his tie and adjusted his messenger bag. "I'm hoping to interview for the position that opened up there."

Hmm… No doubt, he was hoping to interview for her husband's old position.

"Well, good luck." The elevator announced his floor, but she couldn't let the moment pass without teasing him. "My appointment with Ms. Hamilton is not for business, but for pleasure."

He stepped out of the car and spun around. The shocked expression on his face had Raya giggling as the door closed.

She shook her head and stood in the middle of the elevator, waiting for her floor. The doors finally opened and she stepped off, her heels clicking along with the marble floors. Today, making this walk was much different than when she made it with her husband.

Before, it had seemed as if she were arriving for her execution.

Today, she boldly walked with confidence. Her coat flared around her legs while her hips swayed seductively. She made her way to Hadley's office and pushed open the glass door.

The receptionist looked up from her desk and offered Raya a bright smile. Raya's gaze dropped down to read the nameplate.

DON'T TELL ME NO

"Hello, ma'am. How may I help you?" Micah asked. She was a pretty brunette, dressed in a pale pink pant suit and a cream camisole.

"Yes, I have an appointment with Ms. Hamilton. My name is Raya White."

"I'm sorry. Ms. Hamilton's calendar is blocked off this morning for a few hours. She doesn't have any appointments," Micah replied, not bothering to consult her computer.

Raya chuckled and motioned to it.

"I assure you, I have an appointment. Why don't you be a dear and hit a couple buttons on your keyboard and check. Or, you can call Ms. Hamilton yourself to ask her if I'm supposed to be here." Raya folded her hands together in front of her, offering Micah the fakest smile she could muster up.

She wasn't to be dismissed.

Micah rolled her eyes and picked up the phone. Dialing a number, she put it on speakerphone. "Ms. Hamilton, I'm sorry to bother you, but there's a Raya White here saying she has an appointment with you. I didn't have—"

"She does. Why are you calling me? Escort

her in here immediately." Hadley's voice was cold, dripping with power. Raya held back a smirk at the show of Hadley's authority.

It sent an electric current straight to Raya's pussy.

"Yes, ma'am. I'll bring her straight to you." Ending the call, she stood, straightened her jacket, and offered Raya a strained smile. "My apologies. Please, follow me."

Micah led her down a hallway to the familiar double wooden doors that housed Hadley's office.

Micah gave two brisk knocks before opening the door.

"Mrs. White for you, Ms. Hamilton."

"Thank you." Raya brushed past her and into the office. Turning, she gave the pissed off receptionist a smile. "I got the door."

Closing it on Micah's surprised face, she flipped the lock.

Well, that certainly felt good.

Bitch.

"Raya, my darling." Hadley's voice drew her attention. She turned around, leaned back against the door, and gazed at Hadley, who sat in her oversized leather chair, looking as beautiful as she did this morning.

Once before, Raya had been intimidated when entering the room. Now that her gaze swept the area, she saw all of the accomplishments of her lover. Hadley's office showed off her hard work and her impressive career. It was the office of a billionaire technology conglomerate.

"Hello, Hadley," Raya purred. Reaching down, she undid the ties of her jacket and allowed it to fall to the floor. The air-conditioned room caressed her nipples, which beaded into tight little brown buds. Holding onto her purse, she sauntered across the room, feeling like a sexy goddess.

Fire blazed in Hadley's eyes.

Raya arrived at her desk and dropped her purse down onto it.

"It took you forever to get here."

"Did you miss me?" Raya asked, settling down onto her lap.

"You know I did." Grabbing the back of Raya's neck, she kissed her, hard and deep. The kiss went on for what seemed like forever. Hadley's hands were everywhere on Raya: her tits, her thighs, her ass, and her hair.

They pulled back and stared at each other.

Raya felt her heart skip a beat.

She didn't know what this was between them, but whatever it was, it was intense, and the pull to be with Hadley was overwhelming.

Without saying a word, Raya slipped off of Hadley's lap, knelt on the floor before her, and slid her hands underneath her skirt. Hadley stood and unbuttoned her skirt, allowing it to fall to the floor. Soon, her blouse and bra joined the pile.

Hadley sat back in her chair and slid down so her ass rested on the edge. Opening her legs, she placed one on her desk, giving Raya a perfect view of her pretty pink pussy. Quickly dragging her purse onto the floor next to her, she turned her attention back to Hadley.

Slowly, she started with soft, sensual kisses to Hadley's legs, all the way up to her belly, and then between her thighs.

Pressing a kiss to Hadley's slit, she glided her tongue along the edge of it. With her finger, she parted Hadley's folds, revealing her protruding clitoris, and began teasing Hadley with her tongue, tracing the little bundle of nerves.

"Hmm... That feels so good, baby."

Raya sucked the flesh into her mouth with a slight suction. She continued teasing, licking, and sucking Hadley. The taste of her lover exploded on her tongue as Hadley's juices flowed from her core.

Raya licked the entire length of her pussy before leaning away and reaching down into her purse for the dildo she'd brought with her. She had playfully named him Big D. It was a wide cock with a set of balls attached to it.

Hadley chuckled. "Such a naughty girl. I didn't think you took Big D anywhere."

"Today was a special occasion." Gripping the cock in her hand, she returned to eating Hadley out, thinking this was the best lunch break she'd had in a while. She licked and slurped up all of Hadley's cum before teasing her opening with the blunt tip of Big D.

Sitting back on her knees, she worked Big D inside.

"Fuck, Raya," Hadley moaned.

"That's what I'm here for."

She pulled the cock out before sliding it back in, pushing it as far as it would go.

"Ahh!" Hadley cried out as Raya began to

set a rhythm, thrusting the cock deep inside of her.

Raya latched onto Hadley's clit. She could already sense that Hadley wasn't going to last long, which was okay. It would just take the edge off, and the second one wouldn't come on as fast.

"Fuck me harder," Hadley ordered, her voice carrying through the room, but neither of them cared. Raya doubted anyone would dare say anything to the CEO of the company.

Raya did as she was commanded, pounding the dick into her while rubbing her clit.

Hadley quickly reached her orgasm. Her long, drawn-out moan echoed off the walls as her body trembled, her legs up in the air. Pulling Big D out, Raya began lapping up all the juices flowing from Hadley's core.

"That was just what I needed." When her gaze met Raya's, a smile took over her beautiful face. "I hope you brought more toys."

CHAPTER 9

Raya's face rested on Hadley's desk as she spread her ass wide, taking her time feasting.

"Remind me, I have something for you," Hadley murmured.

"Hmm..." was all Raya could muster up. Hadley's talented tongue was currently tracing her dark rim before trailing down to her pussy, ensuring she tasted all of her. Her tongue was everywhere: her pussy, her clit, her ass.

Raya's body was burning with desire. She was so close to coming because of Hadley's unmerciful teasing. Her fingers would brush her clit and rub her for a few seconds before disappearing.

Raya just wanted to grab her hand and

bring it back, demanding she give her an orgasm.

The sound of vibrating caught her attention.

"Stand up." Helping Raya up, she spun her around and kissed her until she could barely stand on her own.

Pulling her toward the window, Hadley pushed her up against it.

The coolness of the glass was a shock to her warm skin. Her hard nipples were pressed against it, sending a shiver down her spine.

"It's cold," Raya giggled as Hadley covered her back with her body, her firm breasts resting against her shoulder blades.

"I want the world to see how beautiful you are." The vibrating noise was getting louder, and she remembered packing a small silver bullet vibrator into her purse. Raya turned her head to offer her lips to Hadley, but Hadley pushed her face toward the window.

"Hadley," Raya moaned.

"Look down at all the people," she ordered, nipping Raya's shoulder. "Imagine them watching us."

Raya did, but they looked like ants scurrying along the sidewalks.

Hadley spread her folds open and pressed the silver bullet against her clit. Her body jerked from the sensation of the vibrations meeting her swollen clit.

"Hadley," she moaned again, her hands resting against the glass, trying to balance herself. Hadley's free hand cupped her tit and squeezed it hard.

"You like having people watch you get fucked, so I'm going to make you cum in front of the entire city." Hadley bit her ear before trailing kisses along her neck and shoulders, her hand rotating from massaging her mound to pinching her nipple.

Her clit was growing more and more sensitive as the vibrations grew stronger. Her knees grew weak. She leaned back against Hadley, panting.

Hadley was everywhere. Her lips, her teeth, hands, and body. She held Raya while her body began to tremble and shake.

She threw her head back, crying out, moaning.

"Come on, baby. Let go," Hadley purred,

pressing the bullet harder against Raya's clit. "Come for me, Raya."

Raya's body detonated.

She screamed, unable to handle the sweet form of torture.

Hadley caught her just as her legs gave out. Wrapping her arms around Raya, she went down with her to the floor, kissing her forehead.

"That's my girl."

Raya turned and kissed her, finally understanding all the feelings she harbored for Hadley.

She wasn't sure when it happened, but she had fallen in love with her.

❦

Raya sat at Hadley's desk while she attended a conference call. Two hours they had locked themselves away in her office, fucking every second of it. On the desk, in front of the window, on her couch. Hell, even the floor.

Hadley had left, leaving Raya with a silly grin on her face and a new pair of diamond earrings in her ears.

She was in love.

In love with Hadley Hamilton.

Where did that leave Brandon?

She didn't know.

What she did know, though, was that she was head over heels in love with Hadley. It was a different love. Now that she thought about it, Brandon was the first person who really gave her attention.

But Hadley was right. She always looked out for him, but did he ever do the same for her?

She didn't need anyone else to answer her.

She knew the answer.

Now Raya was dressed again in her coat, doing the research her laptop wouldn't allow her to do. She was going to have to get a new computer of her own soon.

Running her toes along the cold floor, she wrote down a few of the things she was finding. She had needed to come up with a good background for a priceless painting that was misplaced in the story she was working on. She hadn't realized how much went into the preservation of old art. One internet search led to another, and twenty minutes later, she was finally getting some good stuff to put into her story.

Accidentally minimizing the internet, a folder on Hadley's desktop caught her eye.

B. White.

"What is this?" she murmured. She felt nauseated, because she already knew the file was about her husband.

She knew she shouldn't click on it. This was Hadley's work computer. What if it was someone else with the same first initial and last name as Brandon? White was a common name, and so was the first initial B. There were plenty of names that started with the letter B.

To prove that it had nothing to do with her husband, she clicked on the folder, and what she found gutted her.

Proof of all his thievery. This, Raya already knew about, and still hadn't come to terms with it.

But the rest left her floored.

Her dear husband didn't know how to keep his dick in his pants.

Apparently, he didn't know about the cameras around the building. If he had, he didn't care. Kissing a few random women who'd met him in the building for whatever reasons. Even a video in what looked to be a copier room where she watched him fuck some woman against the wall.

Her stomach clenched as she watched him. She clicked on video after video, finding her unfaithful husband with countless amounts of women.

Raya rarely came to the building.

She shouldn't have to come check on her husband, who was supposed to be loyal to her.

He was only about himself.

Hadley had to have shown Brandon these videos. There was no way she just had them just for the sake of having them.

Raya sat back in the chair, numb.

She didn't know what to do. One thing she knew was that she and Brandon were done. There was nothing he could do or say that could explain any of what she'd seen on the videos.

Tears blurred her vision. She'd done everything she could to make sure she was a good wife to Brandon.

Everything.

And this was how he thanked her?

Now it all made sense why he was looking so haggard, and always asking about Hadley.

He wanted to know if Hadley had disclosed his infidelities.

Raya didn't know how long she sat there staring at the screen.

Hadley's voice broke into her thoughts. "Raya, my love. What's wrong?" A worried look took over her face as she rushed across the room.

"You knew," Raya whispered, pointing to the computer screen.

"Shit." Hadley ran a frustrated hand over her face before kneeling down in front of Raya. "Yes, I knew, and when I found out he stole the money from me, that was the last straw. I knew all about you, Raya. I wanted you. He didn't deserve you."

"Why didn't you just tell me that my husband was cheating on me?"

"Would you have believed me?" She pressed a kiss to the back of Raya's hand. "We really didn't know each other, but I knew from the moment we first met that I wanted to make you mine. Brandon's thievery gave me the edge I needed."

"But the contract?"

"Was my way of getting you to get to know me. I had never planned on using the videos for anything. I did tell Brandon we had them, but it was going to be up to him to tell you of his cheating ways."

"You threatened to throw me in jail with him!" Raya cried out, trying to pull away from Hadley, who held on strong.

"I would have never done that. It was the only way I could ensure you would sign the contract." Hadley grabbed her face. "Think, baby. You know me. Would I have done anything to hurt you? I've done so much to get you to be with me. I want to give you the world."

Her voice broke at the end of her declaration.

Raya stared at her. She was such a strong woman, and to see her on her knees, voice shaky, made Raya take a serious look at her.

"I've never lied to you. If you didn't feel comfortable with anything we did, you could have used your safe word. That was why I gave you one. I wouldn't have forced you to have sex with me, ever."

Raya sniffed, her eyes filling with tears again.

Hadley reached up and pulled Raya's head toward hers, where they rested their foreheads together.

"I've fallen in love with you, Raya White. I want you to be with me because you want to be, and not because of a stupid contract."

Her blue eyes were wide, and Raya saw the truth in them.

A laugh escaped her as she brushed Hadley's hair from her face.

"I love you too, Hadley." Her heart swelled, knowing that Hadley loved her back. She pressed a kiss to Hadley's lips.

"God, that's the best thing I've heard all day. Let's go home, baby. I'll prove how much I love you." Hadley pulled her up from the chair and kissed her sweetly. "Whatever you decide to do with Brandon, just know, you have access to my lawyers. I'll pay for everything."

Raya grinned and threw her arms around Hadley. She wasn't sure what the future was going to hold, but she knew Brandon wasn't going to be a part of it.

"Okay. I'll think of a plan for my cheating ass husband later. I want you to take me home and make me forget everything I saw

DON'T TELL ME NO

on that computer." Gathering her purse, she threw the strap over her shoulder. Just as they turned to leave, the door burst open.

"Where's my wife?" Brandon roared, striding into the room.

"You can't just barge in there!" Micah screamed, racing into the room after him, with a familiar figure entering behind her.

The guy from the elevator.

Raya knew he looked familiar. Now it was coming to her. He was a work friend of Brandon's. His name escaped her at the moment... Lance? Nick? Fuck, she couldn't remember. He must have called Brandon and told him he saw her in the building.

"What the hell is the meaning of this?" Hadley snapped, moving to stand in front of Raya.

"I'm here for my wife," Brandon demanded, stopping in the center of the room. He was dressed in jeans and a dark shirt. His hair was longer than he usually kept it. A shadow of a beard was present, which was definitely not his style.

"Do you want me to call security, Ms. Hamilton?" Micah looked scared, as if this would cost her her job. Deciding on her own,

115

she spun around and walked out the room with her cell phone to her ear.

"You aren't here for anyone. Did you forget the contract that was signed, Brandon?" Hadley stood her ground. Her voice was low, and if Raya wasn't mistaken, she even growled. The woman had bigger balls than most men. It was no wonder she was so successful.

"I'm sure there's a loophole. I'll pay back the money, Hadley," he snarled. Moving around Hadley, he held out his hand. "Let's go, Raya."

Raya stared at it, blinked, and held up her finger. "Hold on."

Walking back over to the computer, she turned the monitor around for the entire room to see.

"Were you thinking of me when you were fucking her?" Raya asked quietly, meeting Brandon's eyes. His Adam's apple bobbed up and down as he swallowed hard. She clicked on another video. "Or how about when you fucked this one?"

"You told me you wouldn't show her those," he growled, swinging to face Hadley. "We had an agreement."

"I didn't. Raya found them on her own, snooping through my computer." Shrugging, the cool businesswoman stared at him. "Now, remove yourself from my building before I have you thrown out."

"Raya…" Brandon ran his fingers through his hair. "Baby, I can explain. Just come home with me—"

"I'm not going anywhere with you," Raya interjected, walking toward Hadley.

"Let's go, Brandon." The elevator guy stepped forward and placed a hand on Brandon's shoulder.

Brandon hollered, "Get off me, Nolan! I'm not going anywhere without my wife!"

Holding up his hands, Nolan backed away.

"Go home, Brandon." It was sad to see her husband fall apart, but she didn't feel sorry for him.

Three burly security officers rushed into the room, each looking as if they were linebackers for a professional football team.

"Is there a problem?" the first one asked.

"Yes, Bill. Mr. White is trespassing. Please escort him off the premises before I decide to press charges."

"Yes, ma'am," Bill said. They encircled

Brandon and pounced on him. He was no match for the three guards. They practically dragged him out of the room, with Nolan following behind him, shaking his head. Brandon's screaming and yelling could be heard through the hall.

"Are you okay?" Pulling Raya to her, Hadley pressed a kiss to her forehead.

"Yes." Raya wrapped her arms around her, resting her head on her shoulder. "Take me home."

EPILOGUE

Raya stretched her arms above her head, basking in the warmth of the sun. Sunbathing naked in Greece while sailing the Mediterranean Sea was a luxury she never thought she would experience. But thanks to Hadley, anything she wanted, she received.

Six months had passed since the day she found out her husband was not only a thief, but an unfaithful wretch. Looking back, it was like she didn't even know the man he had become. So much had changed with him since they had married.

Now, Raya didn't have to worry about him.

With Hadley's lawyer's help, they had a quick divorce, with Raya not being affected by it. She left with everything that was hers, and didn't care about anything else but her dignity. If she had let Hadley do what she wanted, he would have been broke and in jail.

He was a resourceful guy who would eventually get back on his feet, but without Raya. She had moved in with Hadley, and was having the time of her life.

Hadley loved her, took care of her, and ensured her every need and want was met. Not a moment went by that Raya didn't feel her woman's love.

"Enjoying yourself?" Hadley asked, dropping down onto the plush towel next to Raya. She too was naked, looking stunning with her golden tan.

The trip had been Raya's idea. She had never been to Greece or sailed the sea, so Hadley had made it happen. Two weeks of cruising around and touring different countries was a dream of hers come true.

Hadley brought her computer to get in some work each morning, but spent the rest of the day with Raya.

"I'm doing fabulous, lover." Raya ran her hands along her stomach and breasts, cupping them as if to offer them up to the sun god.

"That's what I want to hear," Hadley chuckled. Moving closer to Raya, she pulled her legs open and cupped Raya's pussy with her hand. "I just wanted to check on my pussy to make sure she's doing well too."

"Well, she's missing you," Raya pouted playfully, spreading her legs wide. Her pussy grew slick with need as Hadley bent down and captured one of her breasts with her lips, sucking the mound into her mouth while caressing Raya's thigh.

Raya grew eager to have Hadley make love to her. Her arousal grew even more when Hadley picked up a pink silicone toy, thick and curved at the tip. Slipping it in between Raya's folds, she slowly penetrated her dripping wet pussy.

Methodically, she began to thrust it in and out of Raya.

Hadley released Raya's tit and focused on her core, fucking her with it slowly, leisurely. Raya loved seeing her so relaxed.

Sitting up, she began rubbing Raya's clit with her other hand while the toy plunged deep.

Raya moaned, writhing in ecstasy.

"Your pussy looks so good right now," Hadley purred through a grin, just as the toy's ridid edge brushed against her clit. The sound of her juices gushing out of her filled the air, the sound beautiful to her ears.

Picking up speed, Hadley pumped harder.

Raya concentrated on the sensation of the toy driving inside of her, along with Hadley's fingers rubbing her clit. It was becoming too much.

Thrusting her hips toward Hadley's hands, her back arched and she moaned as her orgasm rushed through her.

"Keep going," Raya gasped. Her hips pumped the air, taking the toy deeper, while Hadley's fingers strummed faster against her clit.

Her body vibrated as another climax slammed into her, her pussy clenching and pulsing around the

"Oh, God, I'm cumming!" Raya slumped down on her towel. Her body still shook slightly while Hadley gently removed the silicone toy from her.

Hadley murmured, "I love watching you

cum," as she leaned down, covering Raya's body with hers, kissing her passionately.

Raya broke the kiss, brushing her nose against Hadley's. "I love cumming because of you. I love you.

"And I love you." Pressing a chaste kiss to her lips, Hadley shifted their position, opening Raya's legs so she could brush her clit against Raya's. "I want to make you cum again."

She rounded her hips, allowing their clits to glide against each other.

Raya smiled, utterly in love. She couldn't deny it. This was the type of love she deserved, and from a woman willing to do whatever she had to do to be with her.

A woman who wanted to cherish her.

Love her always.

She gasped as Hadley thrust a little harder. Raya's clitoris was ultra-sensitive after having two back-to-back orgasms, but with Hadley, that was the norm.

Resting her hands on Hadley's waist, she ground herself against her. She didn't know what the future held, but what she did know was that she wanted to be in Hadley's life.

ABOUT THE AUTHOR

Honey Chanel is an erotic author who loves to dream up sexy fantasies and share them with the world. Her stories are full of sexy scenes that will leave you breathless. She loves to write about kick-ass women who loves to get naughty and dirty.

Sign up for Honey's newsletter HERE.

Follow Honey Chanel on social media:

ALSO BY HONEY CHANEL

Honey Chanel Box Sets

Santa's Naughty Girls: Lesbian Holiday Erotic Romance

Erotic Lesbian Workplace Tales

Her Sexy Valentine

BFF: A Collection of Lesbian Short Stories

The Billionaire Lesbian Club

Maid for Her

There for Her

Always for Her

Lesbian Next Door

Friendly Neighbor

Private Lessons

Nanny Service

Erotic Lesbian Workplace Tales

Assisting the Model

Assisting the Heiress

Assisting the Teacher

Assisting the Chef

Assisting the Lawyer

**Save money and buy the complete boxset HERE!

Single Moms Unleashed Series

Slumber Party

Book Club

Camping Trip

Vacation Trip

Masquerade Ball

Diary of A Lesbian Call Girl Series

Executive Liaison

New Client

Couple's Therapy

V.I.P Client

Match Point

Dirty County Girls Series

Crossing the Line

Weekend Secrets

New Addiction

Pretty Perfection

Printed in Great Britain
by Amazon